Three Brave Women

C. L. G. Martin

Illustrated by

Peter Elwell

Atheneum Books for Young Readers

Text copyright © 1991 by C. L. G. Martin
Illustrations copyright © 1991 by Peter Elwell
Atheneum Books for Young Readers
An imprint of Simon & Schuster
Children's Publishing Division
1230 Avenue of the Americas
New York, New York 10020
Printed and bound in Hong Kong
10   9
The text of this book is set in 16 point Aldus.
The illustrations are rendered in pen-and-ink and watercolor.
Library of Congress Cataloging-in-Publication Data
Martin, C.L.G. Three brave women/C.L.G. Martin;
illustrated by Peter Elwell.   p.   cm.
Summary: Mama and Grammy's humorous childhood anecdotes
help Caitlain come to terms with her fear of spiders.
I S B N   0 - 0 2 - 7 6 2 4 4 5 - 5
[1. Fear—Fiction. 2. Mothers and daughters—Fiction.
3. Grandmothers—Fiction. 4. Spiders—Fiction.]
I. Elwell, Peter, ill. II. Title. III. Title: 3 brave women.
PZ7.M356776Th   1991
[E]—dc20   89-77770   CIP   AC

With love to Jerry,
Tony, and Rikki —
for understanding about spiders
— C.L.G.M.

To Cecilia
— P.E.

"Oooooo! I hate Billy Huxley," Caitlin screeched. "Hate, hate, *hate*!" She threw herself onto the porch swing between Mama and Grammy.

"Caitlin, where are your pants?" Mama asked in quiet surprise.

"On the sidewalk." Caitlin began to sob. "A big, hairy spider was climbing up my leg, so I took them off."

"I see," said Mama, "but why are you crying?"

"Billy Huxley saw my underpants. And they have ducks on them. Billy Huxley saw my duck underpants!" Caitlin buried her face in the swing's plump cushion.

Grammy patted Caitlin's back, Mama smoothed her hair, and Grammy's curly, floppy Muffie bounced onto the porch, dropping Caitlin's pants at her feet. *"Woof!"* she said, waiting for a thank-you.

"Billy Huxley is going to tell everyone that I'm afraid of spiders and that I wear duck underpants. I'm never going outside again." Caitlin sniffled. *"Never!"*

"I know exactly how you feel," Grammy said.
"When I was your age, I spent most of my life locked in the bathroom."

"Why?" Caitlin wiped her wet face on Mama's skirt and pulled on her pants.

"Because my big brothers put worms in my shoes and mice in my bed and spiders in my hair. Then they made fun of me when I got scared."

Caitlin shuddered. Billy Huxley had seen her underpants, but at least he hadn't put a spider in her hair.

Mama was laughing. "Tell Caitlin why they treated you so horribly, Mother."

Grammy started giggling. Caitlin was confused.

"When my brothers wanted to go to a ball game or a social or even on a date, I whined and whined until my mama made them take me along."

"And they threw spiders on you so you wouldn't want to follow them," Caitlin guessed. "Are you still scared of spiders, Grammy?"

"I surely am. Makes my skin crawl just to imagine them."

"How about worms?"

"I've never met a worm that I liked."

"How about mice?"

"Remember the Christmas mouse?" Mama asked.

Caitlin remembered. A blur of fur pulling a long, wormy tail had flashed across the kitchen floor. Before she knew it, Grammy had plunked her down on the table next to the Christmas turkey and climbed up after her.

Mama was having a giggle fit with her memories. "Remember?" she asked, wiping tears from her eyes. "You wouldn't come down till Gramps caught the poor little thing in the wastebasket."

"Now, just a minute, my darling daughter," Grammy said with a wag of her finger. "Caitlin and I are not the only scaredy-cats on this swing.

"I heard this story directly from your daddy, Caitlin, and it's a wonder that you're here to hear it, too."

"Tell me, Grammy."

"Long, long ago, in the years B.C. —"

"Before Caitlin," Caitlin said, interrupting. Grammy started all of her stories that way.

"Before Caitlin," Grammy continued. "Even before Mama and Daddy were married. Daddy took Mama out in his boat for a day of fishing. The sky was blue and the sun was warm and the fish were biting at whatever they dropped in the water. Everything was practically perfect, until...

"Guess what Mama spotted in the boat?"

Caitlin wrinkled her nose. "A spider," she said confidently.

"A huge, black spider—a very close relative of the tarantula," Mama added. "And it started crawling toward me." Her voice rose to a higher pitch. "And when you're in a little boat in the middle of a big lake, there's nowhere to run."

"Easy, Meg," Grammy said, patting Mama's hand. "I'm telling this story."

Caitlin imagined herself in Mama's place. "What happened?" she asked breathlessly.

Grammy went on. "Mama screamed and carried on so that the boat started to rock. Daddy tried to climb up to the front of the boat to kill the spider, but with all the rocking going on he lost his balance and fell down on his brand-new fishing rod."

"Was Daddy hurt?"

"No. But his brand-new fishing rod snapped right in half."

"Daddy didn't talk to me for the rest of the day," Mama added.

"What happened to the spider?" Caitlin wanted to know.

"I don't remember." Mama sighed. "I just wanted to make up with Daddy."

"I'm never gonna make up with Billy Huxley. I hate him, and I'm gonna stay in the house all summer, and I'm not going to school again, either."

"Well," Mama reasoned, "if you stay in all summer, you won't get sunburned, and you won't get water up your nose at the swimming hole, and you won't get so dirty, which means I'll have less laundry to do."

Caitlin pouted. "I wish I could show that Billy Huxley. He thinks he's so great."

"There must be a way," Grammy said.

They thought and thought.

"I know. I'll catch a spider," Caitlin said suddenly.

"Oooooo," Mama and Grammy said together.

"Will you help me?"

Mama and Grammy wrinkled their noses.

"You find a spider," Mama said. "I'll go get a jar."

"And I'll find a stick to catch it on," Grammy added.

Caitlin looked all over the porch and along the basement walls. She looked under the bushes and in the garage. Where were all the big, black spiders when you needed one?

Caitlin searched the dark shadows under the side porch. If there were any big, black spiders around, that's where they'd be.

Mama and Grammy peered over her shoulder.

"Perfect spider hangout," Grammy said, tying her apron over her hair.

Mama gulped and pulled on her garden gloves. "Go ahead, Caitlin. We'll be right behind you."

A chill crept up Caitlin's back. Slowly she poked her head into the musty darkness, walking her hands across the cool mud. Grammy hiked her skirt above her knees and crawled behind, followed by Mama, who sneezed from the dampness.

They ducked their heads and searched the hanging cobwebs — until Caitlin spied the *biggest, blackest* spider in the whole world.

Mama held out the jar with a shaky hand. Grammy raked her stick through the cobwebs till the monster spider dangled from the end, its legs stretching and pawing at the air.

As Grammy lowered the spider into Mama's bobbing jar, the spider climbed higher on its silky web. Grammy tapped the stick against the jar, but the spider wouldn't drop. It climbed still higher on its thread and grabbed hold of the stick.

"Oh-oh," said Grammy.

"Ugh," said Mama.

The spider crawled up the stick toward Grammy's hand.

Caitlin took the lid from Mama and tried to sweep the spider back to the end of the stick. But the hairy, ugly spider ran over the lid and onto Caitlin's hand.

"Oo-oo-oo-oo." Caitlin gasped.

"S-s-steady," Grammy said.

"E-e-easy. " Mama stuttered, too.

The feathery tickle of tiny spider feet brushed over Caitlin's hand. Caitlin clenched her teeth. She wanted to fling her hand toward the darkness, sending the spider flying through the shadows. Then the cool glass jar settled on her arm, and the rough stick scraped gently across her hand. She didn't move.

"There!" cried Mama.

Caitlin slammed the lid on the jar and crawled quickly
after Mama and Grammy, back to the daylight.

Grammy pulled the apron off her hair and rubbed it
across her dirty knees. "We are three brave women,"
she said triumphantly as they all admired their catch
in the jar.

The big spider was trying to climb the slippery cage,
but its long, thin legs slid hopelessly over the glass.

Out in the sunlight the spider didn't look quite so big. It wasn't a bit hairy. And it wasn't even black — its round body was colored in shades of brown and beige that formed a pattern as lacy as a snowflake.

"My," Grammy said, holding the jar close to her face. "This spider is actually quite pretty. Look."

The spider began to run in circles at the bottom of the jar. Then it stopped, still as a rock.

"I think it's confused," said Grammy.

"I think it's tired," said Mama.

"I think it's scared," said Caitlin. "I'm gonna show Billy Huxley. Then I'm gonna let it go."

"That sounds like a good idea," said Grammy. "Would you take Muffie along for her walk?"

Caitlin snapped the leash to Muffie's collar, picked up her spider, and headed for Billy Huxley's house.

Billy Huxley was hunched over his sidewalk, drawing giant chalk bugs on the cement.

Caitlin held out her jar. "Hey, Billy—" But before she could say another word, Billy shot to his feet and jumped inside his front door. Muffie sniffed at the door, wagging her whole body back and forth.

"Go away," Billy said, flattening his nose against the screen door. "I'm busy."

"Well," Grammy called when Muffie pulled Caitlin back into the yard, "was Billy Huxley impressed by your spider?"

"He ran into his house," Caitlin answered.

"He was afraid of your spider?" Mama asked in surprise.

"No." Caitlin giggled.

"What's so funny?" Grammy said.

"Billy Huxley was afraid of Muffie!"

"You don't say!" Mama gasped.

"Grammy, can I take Muffie back over to Billy Huxley's house?"

"Whatever for?"

"I'm gonna make Muffie sit on Billy Huxley till he promises never *ever* to tell anyone about my duck underpants."

"Caitlin McKay!" Grammy cried.

"Then I'm gonna show him how to pet Muffie, so he won't be scared of dogs anymore."

"That's a great idea," said Mama. "And if Billy's not afraid of dogs, then maybe his children won't be afraid of dogs, either."

"Or his grandchildren," added Grammy.

Billy Huxley's grandchildren! This was turning into a pretty important day.

"When I get back, I'm gonna catch a mouse," Caitlin said.

"Oooooo," said Grammy.

"And then I'm gonna dig up some worms."

"Ugh," said Mama.

"Will you help?" Caitlin asked.

"Sure," said Grammy, and Mama wrinkled her nose as she nodded.

"Good," said Caitlin, running after Muffie. "If Billy Huxley's grandchildren aren't gonna be afraid of dogs, then my grandchildren aren't gonna be afraid of *anything*!"